P9-AOA-090

Should We Have GUN CONTROL?

BY MAGGI AITKENS

LERNER PUBLICATIONS COMPANY • MINNEAPOLIS

to my nephew, Lyle Sothern

Copyright © 1992 Lerner Publications Company

Second Printing 1993 includes updated information.

Library of Congress Cataloging-in-Publication Data

Aitkens, Maggi
   Should we have gun control? / Maggi Aitkens.
     p. cm. – (Pro/Con)
   Includes bibliographical references and index.
   Summary: Discusses the controversial issues of whether guns contribute to violence and crime and whether government should regulate private citizens' access to all firearms.
   ISBN 0-8225-2601-8
   1. Gun control – United States – Juvenile literature. 2. Firearms – Law and legislation – United States – Juvenile literature. [1. Gun control. 2. Firearms – Law and legislation.] I. Title. II. Series: Pro/Con (Minneapolis, Minn.)
HV7436.A38 1992
363.3'3'0973–dc20   90-22555
                                        CIP
                                          AC

Manufactured in the United States of America

2   3   4   5   6   7   8   98   97   96   95   94   93

TABLE OF CONTENTS

FOREWORD

If a nation expects to be ignorant and free, . . . it expects what never was and never will be.

Thomas Jefferson

Are you ready to participate in forming the policies of our government? Many issues are very confusing, and it can be difficult to know what to think about them or how to make a decision about them. Sometimes you must gather information about a subject before you can be informed enough to make a decision. Bernard Baruch, a prosperous American financier and an advisor to every president from Woodrow Wilson to Dwight D. Eisenhower, said, "If you can get all the facts, your judgment can be right; if you don't get all the facts, it can't be right."

But gathering information is only one part of the decision-making process. The way you interpret information is influenced by the values you have been taught since infancy–ideas about right and wrong, good and bad. Many of your values are shaped, or at least influenced, by how and where you grow up, by your race, sex, and religion, by how much money your family has. What your parents believe, what they read, and what you read and believe influence your decisions. The values of friends and teachers also affect what you think.

It's always good to listen to the opinions of people around you, but you will often confront contradictory points of view and points of view that are based not on fact, but on myth. John F. Kennedy, the 35th president of the United States, said, "The great enemy of the truth is very often not the lie–deliberate, contrived, and dishonest–

but the myth–persistent, persuasive, and unrealistic." Eventually you will have to separate fact from myth and make up your own mind, make your own decisions. Because you are responsible for your decisions, it's important to get as much information as you can. Then your decisions will be the right ones for you.

Making a fair and informed decision can be an exciting process, a chance to examine new ideas and different points of view. You live in a world that changes quickly and sometimes dramatically–a world that offers the opportunity to explore the ever-changing ground between yourself and others. Instead of forming a single, easy, or popular point of view, you might develop a rich and complex vision that offers new alternatives. Explore the many dimensions of an idea. Find kinship among an extensive range of opinions. Only after you've done this should you try to form your own opinions.

After you have formed an opinion about a particular subject, you may believe it is the only right decision. But some people will disagree with you and challenge your beliefs. They are not trying to antagonize you or put you down. They probably believe that they're right as sincerely as you believe you are. Thomas Macaulay, an English historian and author, wrote, "Men are never so likely to settle a question rightly as when they discuss it freely." In a democracy, the free exchange of ideas is not only encouraged, it's vital. Examining and discussing public issues and understanding opposing ideas are desirable and necessary elements of a free nation's ability to govern itself.

This Pro/Con series is designed to explore and examine different points of view on contemporary issues and to help you develop an understanding and appreciation of them. Most importantly, it will help you form your own opinions and make your own honest, informed decisions.

Mary Winget
Series Editor

THANKS TO THE SPORTSMEN...

THE WHITETAIL DEER NUMBER
IN THE U.S. STANDS AT APPROX.
12 MILLION.
DURING THE FIRST DECADE OF
THE 1900's THE POPULATION WAS
LESS THAN 500,000.
FUNDS CONTRIBUTED BY HUNTERS
(LICENSES AND EXCISE TAXES)
HAVE FINANCED HERD AND
HABITAT MANAGEMENT PRACTICES
THAT PAVED THE WAY FOR
THIS DRAMATIC INCREASE.

INTRODUCTION

It was one of those crisp autumn mornings. The sun shone brightly over the Minnesota countryside, slowly but surely melting the frost that had covered the grass during the night. It seemed as though the warm days of summer would linger on forever in spite of the icy chill in the air. But the flocks of ducks and geese that crowded the sky in their orderly V-shaped formations that morning had already begun their flight from the cold winter days to come.

This was the time of year that 15-year-old Jason liked best. He treasured everything about it–the smell of the air, the squawking birds that disrupted the otherwise perfect silence, and, most of all, the chance to go hunting with his father. That morning he crouched next to his father in a **duck blind** near a swampy area. With gun training courses and his father's guidance, Jason had learned how to use guns safely and had become an excellent marksman.

Jason's father is one of the 33 million Americans who own firearms for hunting. But hunting is not the only reason why so many people in the United States buy firearms. Millions of people participate in organized shooting compe-

titions, gun clubs, and other recreational programs. Many others collect firearms as a hobby, the same way some people collect stamps or coins. About three-fourths of all gun owners keep firearms, in part, for protection against criminals.[1]

In the United States, approximately 200 million firearms are in private hands[2] and at least one firearm is found in about half of all U.S. homes[3]. In fact, firearms are in such high demand that every 13 seconds a firearm of one type or another is manufactured for sale in this country.[4]

While most of these firearms are owned by law-abiding citizens, like Jason and his father, a large number of criminals in this country also own guns. For example, on that same autumn day, while Jason and his father were hunting, a 35-year-old man named Joe was parking his car in a crowded section of Chicago, Illinois. If he hurried, he would have just enough time to make it to his daughter's piano recital. He quickly got out of his car, but just as he was locking the door, he felt a pointed object press firmly against his back. It was a handgun. The man holding it demanded Joe's money and the keys to his car. Joe, a tall, muscular man, turned to defend himself. Before he could realize the danger of his situation, the criminal fired and killed him.

This type of incident, in which a firearm is used to murder a person, is not rare in the United States. In fact, the U.S. has the highest firearm murder rate of any democracy in the world. Between 1960 and 1980 in the United States, the number of people murdered by firearms rose 160 percent, compared to an increase of 85 percent for people who were murdered by other means.[5]

Gun-related accidents and suicides must also be considered. Every day in the United States, 10 children ages 18 and under are killed by handguns–mainly by accident–and another 100 children are seriously injured.[6] In addition to those deaths and injuries, a teenager intentionally takes his or her own life with the use of a handgun every three hours.[7]

Most people agree that there is far too much violence and crime in the United States. And almost everyone agrees that something must be done to prevent it. The question is "What?" Are guns the problem, or are people the problem? That is an important issue in the gun control debate.

Before looking at the debate surrounding the issue of gun control, acquaint yourself with the terms for a few types of firearms referred to throughout this book.

- **Handguns** are guns that can be aimed and fired with one hand, as compared to long guns that require additional support. In most states, individuals who wish to buy a handgun simply sign a federal form saying they are not criminals, minors, **illegal aliens,** drug addicts, or mentally ill.
- **Semiautomatic firearms** are guns that fire one bullet per trigger pull. Although some states apply tighter restrictions, under current federal law, semiautomatic firearms can be purchased instantly over the counter.
- **Fully automatic firearms** are guns that fire continuously when the trigger is depressed. Under current federal law, fully automatic weapons must be registered. In 1986 Congress halted the manufacture and sale of new machine guns for civilian use, essentially freezing the number of such guns.
- **Assault firearms** are semiautomatic and fully automatic weapons.[8] Because many assault weapons are designed for military purposes, they are often equipped with combat hardware, such as folding stocks, flash suppressors, and bayonet studs (see p. 12), which are not found on traditional sporting guns. A major problem in drafting legislation to control assault weapons is the difficulty of defining which firearms belong in this category, particularly with respect to semiautomatic firearms. The Senate voted to ban those firearms shown on page 11. However, a similar bill was defeated in the House of Representatives in 1991.

In the United States, the term *gun control* means government regulation of the possession and use of firearms by private citizens. The government regulates firearm manu-

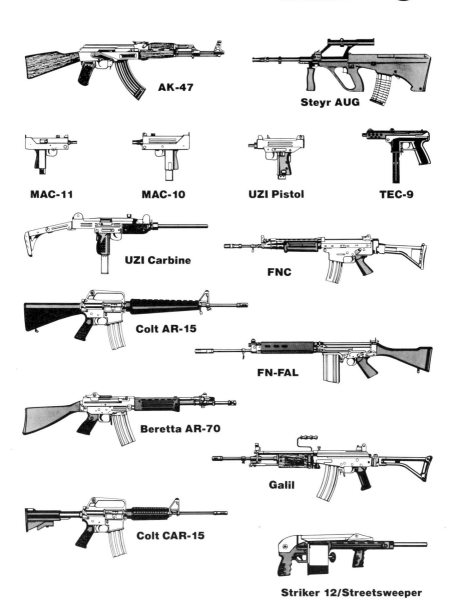

AK-47

Steyr AUG

MAC-11

MAC-10

UZI Pistol

TEC-9

UZI Carbine

FNC

Colt AR-15

FN-FAL

Beretta AR-70

Galil

Colt CAR-15

Striker 12/Streetsweeper

The Senate voted to ban these weapons in the 1989 Anti-drug, Assault Weapons Limitation Act. In 1991, a similar bill was defeated in the House of Representatives, so the ban did not become law. Such weapons are still legal.

Combat Hardware Commonly Found on Assault Weapons

FLASH SUPPRESSOR
Reduces the flash from
the barrel of the weapon,
allowing the shooter to
remain concealed when
shooting at night

BARREL LENGTH
Shorter barrels sacrifice
accuracy and range for
mobility in close combat.

FOLDING STOCK
Designed for concealabil-
ity and mobility in combat
situations

BAYONET STUD
Designed to accommo-
date a bayonet. Serves no
sporting purpose.

**HIGH CAPACITY
DETACHABLE
MAGAZINE**
Permits shooter to fire
dozens of rounds of
ammunition without
reloading

PISTOL GRIP
Helps stabilize the
weapon during rapid fire

facture, possession, and use by passing laws in the U.S.
Congress. Many Americans oppose gun control. They believe that more laws will restrict law-abiding citizens from
using firearms for their enjoyment and security. Many other
Americans, however, favor more gun control laws. These
people believe that limiting the ownership and use of firearms will help reduce not only crimes involving guns, but
also the large number of gun-related accidents and suicides
that occur every year. Both groups have organizations that
represent their views.

Handgun Control, Inc., a non-profit citizens' organization that favors gun control, was founded in 1974 by Dr. Mark Borinsky. Handgun Control, Inc., works to pass federal legislation, or laws, to keep handguns out of the wrong hands. Claiming more than one million supporters, the organization's goal is to establish an effective national gun policy. Members of this organization believe that enacting more gun control laws and enforcing stiffer penalties for criminals who use guns will help reduce gun-related crimes in the United States.

The organization's goals include laws that would require:

- *a waiting period and background check* to screen handgun purchasers and prevent guns from being sold to convicted **felons** and drug users;
- *a ban on the manufacture and sale of snub-nosed handguns* (those with very short barrels), which, according to Handgun Control, Inc., are used in two-thirds of handgun crime;
- *a ban on the sale of military-style assault weapons;*
- *a mandatory jail sentence* for using a handgun while committing a crime;
- *a special license to carry a handgun outside one's home or place of business.*[9]

To accomplish its goals, Handgun Control, Inc. supports political candidates and elected officials who favor gun control laws. The organization also works with members of Congress and state legislators to draft handgun control legislation. Handgun Control, Inc., also conducts research on handgun laws, and its members make appearances on television and radio programs to promote handgun control.

Members of the National Rifle Association (NRA), however, oppose more gun control laws. Most NRA members agree that something must be done to reduce crime, but their position is that gun control does not mean crime control. Instead, they want society to focus on the criminals who commit crimes rather than on the weapons they use. National Rifle Association members believe the solution to violent crime lies in the swift, sure punishment of people who use guns to commit crimes. They think such punishment could occur and be effective if the more than 20,000 currently existing state gun control laws were enforced.

The National Rifle Association, founded in 1871, has nearly 3 million members, 525 full-time employees, and an annual budget of about $88 million.[10] It is one of America's most powerful lobbies, groups that try to influence public officials and affect laws that are passed. The NRA has been highly effective in mobilizing thousands of gun owners into action against gun control legislation. Lobbying, advertisements, letter-writing campaigns, and contributions to political candidates who oppose gun control have been some of the organization's most effective tactics in its fight against tighter firearms laws.

Most NRA members believe that restricting firearms to prevent gun-related deaths is ridiculous. Allen R. Hodgkins III is a spokesperson for the association. During a telephone conversation with the author, he said, "If you follow that logic, we should also ban the use of motor vehicles. More than 47,000 people die each year in motor vehicle accidents. If we ban their use, no one will ever have a motor vehicle accident and no one will ever die."

The idea of restricting firearms can seem absurd when, according to information published by the National Rifle

For many people, guns provide recreation and a sense of satisfaction as skills are developed.

Association, over 99.8 percent of firearms and 99.6 percent of handguns will never be involved in criminal activity.[11] That means that gun control laws will restrict law-abiding citizens, while doing nothing to reduce crime.

But Susan Whitmore, a spokesperson for Handgun Control, Inc., sees it differently. During an interview she said, "We have laws for people who drive cars, including who can drive, how they drive, and under what circumstances. People are required to pass a test, obtain a license, and register their vehicles. They're prohibited from driving while under the influence of drugs or alcohol–when most car accidents occur–and these laws are strictly enforced. We're not calling for a total ban on firearms. We're calling for national laws that stop criminal access to handguns and ensure the appropriate use of firearms–the same way laws require people to use an automobile appropriately. In a country where cars, dogs, and even bicycles must be registered in most areas, shouldn't we have at least similar laws for something as dangerous as firearms?"[12]

According to Whitmore, no one in her organization believes gun control laws alone will stop all handgun violence. "We're not that naive," she says. "The fact is, gun control is only part of the answer–but it's a very important part. We believe it will make a significant dent in the number of needless handgun and other firearm deaths in this country."

To sum up the debate, it's clear that everyone favors crime reduction. But while the National Rifle Association prefers to focus on laws that punish criminals who use guns, Handgun Control, Inc., prefers to punish criminals *and* enact laws that limit people's ownership and use of guns. This strategy, members of Handgun Control, Inc. believe, will address the problem of gun-related accidents, suicides, and crimes *before* they happen. The National Rifle Association, on the other hand, believes that it is unfair to limit people's use of firearms before a gun owner has caused a problem. People should be assumed innocent until they are proven guilty.

The battle between the two organizations takes place on two important fronts. On one front is the question of whether the Second Amendment of the United States Constitution guarantees our right as individuals to own and use firearms as we wish. If it does, gun control laws are basically unconstitutional. On the second front is the question of whether gun control laws really reduce gun-related deaths. If they don't, what's the point of having them?

GUNS IN A BRAVE NEW WORLD

Have you ever gone to an art museum and stood so close to a painting that all you could see was a small area of the canvas with brush strokes and splashes of color? If you have, you know that you needed to take a few steps back from the painting to see the actual picture–the painting as a whole. The issue of gun control in the United States is in some ways like a large painting. In order to fully understand it, you need to step back for a moment–in this case, into the colonial period of American history–to see the whole picture.

Life in the Colonies

When the first European settlers came to this country many years ago, they found a world different from the one we live in now. In fact, it was very different from the societies they had left behind. The early colonists had only minimal comforts. Although the colonists grew some of their food, they also hunted in order to provide themselves with enough to eat. They also had to protect themselves against wild animals. Guns were important to their survival.

Gradually, more and more Europeans arrived on the shores

As the number of colonists increased, so did the violence between them and the Native Americans.

of America. Although the majority were British, others came from different countries and some spoke different languages. One of things they shared was the struggle to survive in the New World.

At first, most Native Americans accepted the colonists and their strange ways. They taught the colonists about the land, farming techniques, and hunting. However, the colonists claimed more and more land, cleared forests, and built towns on land that had belonged to the Native Americans. As the number of colonists grew, so did the differences between them and the Native Americans. Violence between Native Americans and Anglo-European settlers began as early as the 1620s in Virginia and recurred throughout the colonial years. The colonists needed to protect themselves and what they thought of as *their* land from the Native Americans. Guns became important to the colonists for protection.

No one questioned the colonists' right to carry guns. In fact, in some colonies every able-bodied man was *required* to carry a firearm. To protect themselves against outside threats, most of the colonies formed their own militias–organized, military forces called only in times of emergency. The militia included most of the men within a colony. These citizen-soldiers could be called to service at any time to defend the colony, and they were required to provide their own firearms. Once the enemy was defeated, the militia was disbanded.

Guns were an integral part of daily life for the early colonists. These pilgrims are on their way to church.

The American Revolution

Until the middle of the 1700s, colonial pioneers had been more or less ignored by England and other European countries. They enjoyed a large degree of freedom and paid few, if any, taxes. Communication between the colonies and England took several months by ship, so the colonists were used to making their own decisions rather than waiting for permission from England.

But something happened that changed that situation. George III, the king of England, needed money to pay war debts. To raise money, he increased colonial taxes and stationed troops in the colonies to enforce English rule. King George tried to manage the colonies for England's benefit, with little regard for what the colonists wanted.

Tensions mounted between the colonies and England throughout the 1770s. The colonists resented the new taxes, the presence of the king's army on their soil, and the fact that colonists had no voice in decisions made in England that directly affected them. When the colonists began to rebel, King George III responded with an order to his armies and colonial governors to disarm the colonists. He also banned the export of arms and ammunition from England to the colonies.

Colonial Americans knew what it meant to be disarmed. To them the loss of firearms was a loss of liberty. It wasn't the first time that a king of England had taken such measures to guard his power. Henry VII had outlawed hunting in 1485 for the specific purpose of discouraging rebellion among the lower classes. If people had guns for hunting, Henry reasoned, they could also use them to rebel against the king. Later, in 1670, Charles II passed a law that banned all

Patrick Henry, standing front, center, concluded his famous speech with the words "Give me liberty, or give me death," which later became the war cry of the American Revolution.

English people, except some wealthy landowners, from owning firearms.

The colonists were not about to let this happen to them. In one of the most famous speeches in American history, statesman Patrick Henry summed up the situation when he spoke before a Virginia Provincial Convention in March 1775:

> "A well-regulated militia, composed of gentlemen and yeomen [farmers], is the natural strength and only security of a free government....Three million people, armed in the holy cause of liberty, ... are invincible by any force which our enemy can send against us." [1]

Henry ended his speech with the words, "Give me liberty, or give me death." He was ready to fight the British.

The Continental Congress adopted the Declaration of Independence on July 4, 1776. In this painting by American artist John Trumbull, the president of the Congress, John Hancock, sits at the right. Standing in front of him, left to right, are John Adams, Roger Sherman, Robert Livingston, Thomas Jefferson, and Benjamin Franklin, the five committee members named to draft the Declaration.

The New Government

On July 4, 1776, John Adams, Benjamin Franklin, and several other Americans sat quietly in a small room in Philadelphia. They listened to Thomas Jefferson read a long document that the group had been working on for weeks, the Declaration of Independence. In it, the colonists declared their independence from England.

England, however, was not about to give up that vast territory without a fight, and so the American Revolution began. In 1783, after seven years of fighting, the Continental Army, with the support of well-organized colonial militias, defeated the mighty British army, and the United States of America was born.

To make sure the states remained united, representatives from each state met in 1787 to draft the U.S. Constitution.

It took four long months to draft the document, but the work was worth the effort. The government those men formed and the Constitution they created more than 200 years ago are still in place today.

The government of the United States is made up of the president, two houses of Congress, and the Supreme Court. The federal government was given the power to collect taxes, coin and borrow money, regulate trade, declare war, and pass laws for the entire country. Other powers were given to the people and to the individual states to govern themselves.

States were given so much power because early on, each state was viewed as a little country. Americans saw themselves more as part of the state in which they lived than of the United States as a whole. What's more, the people wanted to control the government rather than have the government control them, as had been the case under British rule. Many colonists felt that state governments, because they were smaller and closer to home, would be easier to control than a large national government.

King George III tried to impose English rule on the colonies. The colonists rebelled.

This soldier from the American Revolution is priming the frizzen of his gun.

Even so, Article 1, Section 8 of the Constitution gives Congress the power "to raise and support armies, ... to provide for calling forth the militia to execute the laws of the Union ...," and also "to provide for organizing, arming, and disciplining the militia" in specific situations. The federal government's power to organize an army concerned many citizens. They worried that the federal government would one day create a standing army, a permanent army of paid soldiers, just as England had done. A standing army, they thought, could take away the people's rights. Most people wanted each state to maintain its own militia. Each state would then be able to defend itself from a possible threat from the federal government or even from other states.

Noah Webster (writer, educator, and author of *Webster's Dictionary*) helped persuade people to accept the Constitution by arguing that a national standing army was not a

The American Revolution represented freedom in general, not just freedom from British control. Citizens wanted the right to make their own political and religious decisions.

threat. "Before a standing army can rule," he said, "the people must be disarmed, as they are in almost every kingdom in Europe. The supreme power in America cannot enforce unjust laws... because the whole body of the people are armed, and constitute a force superior to any band of regular troops that can be, on any pretense, raised in the United States."[2]

Nonetheless, it was necessary to make a few additions to the Constitution before all the states would accept it. These additions, or amendments, were written in the form of another document called the Bill of Rights.

The Second Amendment in the Bill of Rights covered one of the main concerns of those early Americans. It states that: "A well-regulated militia, being necessary to the security of a free state, the right of the people to keep and bear arms shall not be infringed."

Is "the right of the people to keep and bear arms" limited to a militia, or does it include gun ownership and use by private citizens?

THE SECOND
AMENDMENT

If people didn't have language, we would have a very difficult time making ourselves understood, and we would often be confused about what people tried to tell us. But sometimes language can be confusing too, because words can mean different things to different people. Take the word *family*, for example. To you, it may mean your parents, brothers, sisters, cousins, aunts, uncles, and everyone else to whom you are related. To your friends, on the other hand, the word *family* may mean just the people with whom they live.

The words used in the Second Amendment cause the same kind of confusion. The amendment says: *A well-regulated militia, being necessary to the security of a free state, the right of the people to keep and bear arms, shall not be infringed.* Although the amendment is not long–only 27 words–people have spent years arguing about what these words mean and what the people who wrote them more than 200 years ago intended the words to mean.

Even the United States Supreme Court–whose duty it is to determine whether laws established by federal, state, and local governments follow the general rules stated in the Constitution–has not been able to put an end to the argument. The exact meaning of the Second Amendment is still unclear.

The debate about gun control begins with the Second Amendment. Does the amendment guarantee individuals the right to own and carry guns for personal use? Some people say it does, and, as a result, they say gun control regulation is illegal because it violates the Constitution. Others, however, interpret the words differently. They say the Second Amendment guarantees each state the right to create its own militia and to use guns for *military* purposes only. This group says that private ownership of guns is not protected by the Constitution, and, as a result, gun control regulation is legal.

To understand the debate about the Second Amendment, we need to look not only at the words the authors of the amendment used, but also at what they *intended* to say. Remember that the Second Amendment was written in 1789–a time when citizens identified more with the state in which they lived (Virginia or New York, for example) than they did with the country as a whole. Because the colonists believed that the English government had abused their rights, they distrusted a large, national government. That's why, when the Constitution was written, the men who wrote it gave many powers to the state governments and limited the powers of the federal government. That's also why the writers of the Constitution decided that instead of having a permanent national militia, each state could create its own militia. In this way, each state could defend itself against the federal government if necessary. The state militias were made up of every able-bodied man in the state. When called to service at the time of war, each man would bring his own firearm.

The Word Game

Of the 27 words in the Second Amendment, two words–*militia* and *people*–seem to cause the most confusion. Supporters of gun control argue that the first part of the Second Amendment–"A well-regulated militia, being necessary to the security of a free state"–means that each state has the right to create its own state militia, such as the National Guard. The second part–"the right of the people to keep and bear arms may not be infringed"–means the people of the state may keep and bear arms to protect the security of the state–in other words, for military purposes. The Second Amendment, in their opinion, does not guarantee individuals the right to privately own guns for any purpose other than a military one.

Most people who oppose gun control regulation insist that the Second Amendment does protect an individual's right to privately own guns for many purposes besides protecting the security of the state. They say the words "people" and "militia" both mean all Americans *as individuals.* They point out that the phrase "the right of the people" is also used in both the First and Fourth Amendments, which guarantee the rights to free speech, assembly, and petition, as well as protection against unreasonable searches and seizures. In those amendments, "the right of the people" has always been interpreted to mean the right of individuals, so why should it have a different meaning in the Second Amendment?

With respect to the word *militia*, those opposed to gun control argue that state militias in 1789 were made up of citizens–specifically, every able-bodied man. Since these citizen-soldiers were required to supply their own firearms

Members of the National Guard are supplied with firearms. There is no longer a need for individuals to own their own weapons for military reasons.

when called to service, the authors of the Second Amendment intended to protect the individual right of every citizen (or at least every able-bodied man) to keep and carry a firearm. Without that right for each *individual*, how could the state defend itself against the federal government?

Those who favor gun control regulation respond that even though it was once necessary for soldiers to supply their own weapons in the event of war, that is no longer true in the United States. Now, our state militias and the United States military supply soldiers with firearms. Since there is no longer a military reason to keep a gun at home, they argue, privately owned guns are not protected by the amendment.

Some people agree in part with both sides of the gun control argument. They say that the Second Amendment actually guarantees *two* rights—not just one. The first is the right of states to form well-regulated militias or a National

Guard, and the second is the right of the people as individuals to keep and bear privately owned arms. If this is true, the government probably does not have the right to pass gun control laws because it would violate that second right.

Still others draw a finer line when it comes to interpreting the Second Amendment. They argue that the amendment gives states the right to form well-regulated militias or a National Guard and that people as individuals have the right to keep and carry certain types of guns–namely, the kinds of guns used by soldiers in state militias. All other guns, such as sawed-off shotguns, can be regulated by the government because such guns have never been used by the military and therefore do not have a military purpose.

Representing the President's Commission on Organized Crime, James D. Harmon, Jr., holds up a sawed-off shotgun during federal hearings on drug trafficking.

The Supreme Court Rules

Federal, state, and local governments all have the power to make laws regulating the ownership and use of guns. Federal laws apply to everyone living in the United States, while state laws–such as those made in New York–apply only to the people living within that state. Local laws are made by county, city, town, and village governments and apply only to people living within those communities. In cases where federal, state, and local laws conflict, federal law takes precedence over state law, and state law takes precedence over local law. In other words, laws enacted at the federal level cannot be ignored or weakened by state or local governments. When court cases involve a conflict between the interpretation of local or state laws and federal laws, the Supreme Court of the United States makes the final decision.

Most of the amendments in the Bill of Rights do apply to the states. This means that all Americans–no matter where they live–are guaranteed the rights listed in the federal Constitution. State governments cannot diminish or eliminate those rights.

The exception to this rule, however, is the Second Amendment, which was written to protect the states against encroachment by the federal government. As a result, each state government has the authority to guarantee, deny, or limit the right of its citizens to keep and bear arms as the state sees fit.

In the few Second Amendment cases the Supreme Court has considered, it has refused to take a position on the amendment's exact meaning. The Court has, however, ruled on five Second Amendment cases.

State Court System

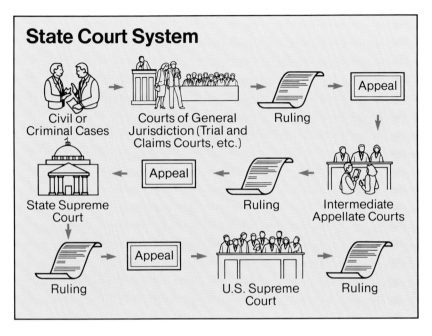

Civil or Criminal Cases

Courts of General Jurisdiction (Trial and Claims Courts, etc.)

Ruling

Appeal

State Supreme Court

Appeal

Ruling

Intermediate Appellate Courts

Ruling

Appeal

U.S. Supreme Court

Ruling

Federal Court System

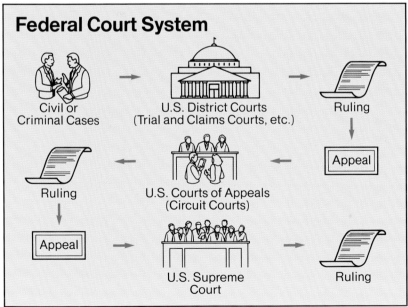

Civil or Criminal Cases

U.S. District Courts (Trial and Claims Courts, etc.)

Ruling

Appeal

Ruling

U.S. Courts of Appeals (Circuit Courts)

Appeal

U.S. Supreme Court

Ruling

United States v. Cruikshank et al. (1875)

In 1874, a group of white men from Louisiana disarmed and murdered two black citizens, Levi Nelson and Alexander Tillman, also from Louisiana. Nelson and Tillman had been on their way to an election or a political meeting preceding an election. The group was accused of 32 counts, or charges, of conspiracy to interfere with the constitutional rights of Nelson and Tillman. Although it was a minor part of the conspiracy charge, one of the accusations against the group was their intent "to hinder and prevent" Nelson's and Tillman's right to bear arms. A jury had found the group guilty of most of the charges, but the case was appealed to the **circuit court.** The accused men argued that what they had done did not violate the laws of the United States. They thought the charges against them were too vague and general for them to plead and prepare their defense. The opinions of the judges on the circuit court were divided. The presiding circuit court judge said that the accusations against the group of men were not charges that were covered by the laws of the United States at that time. He thought only state laws applied to the case.

The *Cruikshank* case focused mostly on the right to vote and the rights of assembly and free speech. The Supreme Court, however, also ruled on the rights guaranteed by the Second Amendment–an individual's right to bear arms for a lawful purpose. The *United States v. Cruikshank* was the first case regarding the Second Amendment ever to come before the United States Supreme Court.[1] In its decision, the Court stated that:

> This is not a right granted by the Constitution. Neither is it in any manner dependent upon that instrument

[the Constitution] for its existence. The second amendment declares that it [this right] shall not be infringed;
but this...means no more than that it shall not be
infringed by Congress. This is one of the amendments
that has no other effect than to restrict the powers of
the national government....[2]

This decision has been interpreted in a few different ways.
Some people believe that the Second Amendment was
written simply to prevent the national government from
taking away a citizen's right to bear arms. Another interpretation is that, although the federal government cannot
restrict the possession of firearms, states can restrict or even
ban the possession of firearms.

Those who favor gun control regulation, however, say the
passage in the *Cruikshank* decision clearly confirms what
they have always believed: that the Second Amendment
does not grant individuals the right to bear arms.

Presser v. Illinois (1886)

The Supreme Court addressed the power of state governments in relation to the Second Amendment at the end of
the 19th century. The case arose when Herman Presser
formed a paramilitary organization (a group resembling
but not actually a part of the military) of 400 men. Mounted
on horseback and equipped with rifles, the group paraded
down the streets of Chicago, Illinois. Presser's men did so,
however, without a license "to conduct military training
when armed," as required under Illinois law. Presser was
promptly arrested, convicted, and charged $10 for his mis-
deed. He appealed the decision, based on the claim that
Illinois law violated his right to keep and bear arms (for
military purposes) under the Second Amendment.

The case made its way to the United States Supreme Court, which **upheld** the decision of the Illinois court. The U.S. Supreme Court determined that the Illinois law did not violate the Second Amendment because, as found in the *Cruikshank* case, the Second Amendment "is only a limitation upon the power of Congress and the National government, and not upon that of the States." The Court also decided that the Second Amendment only protects state militias from being disarmed. Presser, in the court's opinion, was not a state militia because his group of men were not "under the control of the [state] government."[3]

Miller v. Texas (1894)

One day in Texas in 1892, a man named Franklin Miller was convicted of murder by a Texas court and sentenced to

Justices Gray, Jackson, Field, Brown, Fuller (Chief Justice), Chiras, Harlan, White, and Brewer, the 1894 Supreme Court

death. It was against the law in Texas at the time to carry firearms, and any person who did so could be arrested without a warrant, a document that authorizes an officer to make an arrest. Miller didn't argue against the murder conviction. Instead, hoping to weaken the case against him, Miller argued that the Texas law against carrying firearms was unconstitutional. He appealed the state court's decision to the Supreme Court, stating that his constitutional rights under both the Second and Fourth Amendments had been violated in the process of his arrest. (The Fourth Amendment guarantees that "the right of the people to be secure in their persons, houses, papers, and effects, against unreasonable searches and seizures, shall not be violated....) The Supreme Court upheld the lower court's decision stating once again that the Second Amendment only restricts the federal government from disarming state militias and that the Texas firearms laws did not violate the Constitution.[4]

United States v. Miller (1939)

It wasn't until 1939 that the United States Supreme Court heard another case involving the Second Amendment. But this time, the issue was different. The Court ruled on whether the Second Amendment guaranteed the right to keep and bear a certain *type* of firearm.

The matter began when Jack Miller and Frank Layton were arrested while traveling from Claremore, Oklahoma, to Siloam Springs, Arkansas, with a double-barreled, sawed-off, 12-gauge shotgun. Miller and Layton had neglected to register the weapon or to pay the $200 tax required by the National Firearms Act of 1934 before transporting the shotgun across state lines.

When Miller and Layton pleaded that the National Firearms Act of 1934 violated their Second Amendment rights, the lower court agreed and dismissed the charges. The United States appealed the case, however, and the Supreme Court found that the National Firearms Act did not violate the Constitution. The Court stated that:

> In the absence of any evidence tending to show that possession or use of a "shotgun having a barrel of less than eighteen inches [46 centimeters] in length" at this time has some reasonable relationship to the preservation or efficiency of a well-regulated militia, we cannot say that the Second Amendment guarantees the right to keep and bear such an instrument. Certainly it is not within judicial notice that this weapon is any part of the ordinary military equipment or that its use could contribute to the common defense.[5]

Unlike the earlier cases, this case focused on the type of firearm involved, although the Court did not impose an absolute ban on sawed-off shotguns. This Supreme Court decision suggests that, while the federal government cannot regulate the right to keep and bear arms for military purposes, it can regulate the possession of all firearms that are unsuitable for military use. According to some lawmakers and historians, this case suggests that individuals do have the right to keep and bear arms provided they show those arms have some "reasonable relationship to the efficiency of a militia."[6] If this is true, some people wonder whether regulating the ownership of short-barreled shotguns and machine guns is still constitutional since these weapons were sometimes used during World War I and the Vietnam War.[7] Should American citizens be allowed to own any weapon that might be used in a 1990s militia?

Above, *two Morton Grove residents who supported their local ban on handguns;* below, *NRA headquarters in Washington, D.C.*

Quilici v. Village of Morton Grove
(532 F. Supp. 1169, 1981)

The only other case involving the Second Amendment that got as far in the legal appeals process as the Supreme Court never actually came before the Court.

On June 8, 1981, Morton Grove, Illinois, a suburb of Chicago, became the first town in the United States to totally ban the possession of privately owned handguns. Four gun owners took the matter to court. In *Quilici v. Village of Morton Grove*, they argued that under Illinois law individuals have the right to keep and bear arms. The Illinois constitution reads: "Subject only to police power, the right of the individual citizen to keep and bear arms shall not be infringed" (Section 22 of the Illinois constitution).

The district court and the court of appeals ruled that the ban on handguns did not violate the Illinois constitution because the law did not ban all guns, only handguns. The courts also ruled that local governments had the power to

This is a display of some of the illegal weapons seized in raids by agents of the Bureau of Alcohol, Tobacco and Firearms.

These soldiers, performing Basic Training exercises, carry weapons owned by the U.S. government, not by the soldier.

restrict or prohibit the right to keep and bear handguns. When the decision of the lower courts was appealed, the Supreme Court refused to hear the case. As a result, the lower court's decision stood.

The ban on handguns was upheld again on October 19, 1984, by the Illinois Supreme Court in *Kaloimos v. Village of Morton Grove* (53 LW 2233). The court concluded that:

> Because of the comparative ease with which handguns can be concealed and handled, a ban on handguns could rationally have been viewed as a way of reducing the frequency of **premeditated** violent attacks as well as unplanned criminal shootings in the heat of passion or an over-reaction to fears of assault, accidental shootings by children or by adults..., or suicides. The ordinance is a proper exercise of the police power.

Have Times Changed?

The United States Constitution and Bill of Rights have guaranteed Americans' rights for more than 200 years. If the Second Amendment really does mean that every individual in the United States has the right to own any type of firearm, some historians, lawmakers, and supporters of gun control feel that it may be time to change the 200-year-old amendment.

Times have changed, they argue. The authors of the Second Amendment certainly never imagined sawed-off shotguns, or semi- or fully automatic assault weapons. If individuals have the right to own any kind of firearm (or even those used just for military purposes), does this mean we all have the right to install nuclear warheads in our backyards? A line has to be drawn somewhere, they argue.[8]

Likewise, those who wrote the Second Amendment probably did not foresee a time when people would hunt for sport rather than food, or a time when most Americans would have the protection of a large, well-armed police force. Some people argue that, for all practical purposes, we no longer need guns to feed or protect ourselves.[9]

Also, those who wrote the Constitution could not predict how well the government they created would work or how "united" the United States would become. People who oppose gun control regulations argue that if citizens are disarmed, we will lose our basic right to protect "the security of a free state."[10] Others argue that it is no longer necessary to protect that security because there is no longer a threat by the federal government or neighboring states. We have many channels to give people power over the government, such as elections and the court system. During the past 200 years, these systems have been very effective.[11]

Perhaps most important, the United States military is one of the most powerful militias in the world, and it is armed by the government rather than by citizens. Our nation's founders almost certainly, did not imagine a time when each male citizen would not have to carry his own musket (a large gun carried by the infantry) into war. Yet, opponents of gun control say "those who argue that the U.S. armed forces and the National Guard–both standing armies, whose weapons are owned by the federal government and not by the soldier–now take the place of the militia have a sense of confidence in standing armies and in the rulers that . . . [some would consider] naive."[12] In other words, many gun control opponents still see a possible threat to an unarmed citizenry from a centralized government with a standing army.

Finally, the authors of the Second Amendment never foresaw the day when people would live in crowded urban areas, and more than 638,900 violent crimes would be committed each year in this country with handguns alone.[13] Proponents of gun control argue that the time has come to limit this needless killing with firearms through an effective national gun control policy.

Not everyone accepts that argument, however. People on the other side of the issue argue that guns don't kill, people do. Crimes will continue to be committed–with or without gun control regulations. But that's getting ahead of ourselves. Let's first look at existing U.S. gun control laws and then at one of the major questions in this debate: Do guns contribute to crime and violence in this country?

Do gun control laws benefit or restrict private, law-abiding citizens?

GUN CONTROL LAWS

Gun control laws, which restrict the possession and use of firearms, are not new. In fact, one of the first English laws on record, from the ninth century, prohibited people from drawing a weapon in the king's hall or at a public meeting, lending a weapon for purposes of murder, or using another's weapon to commit a crime.[1] Some early gun control laws were aimed at protecting people's safety. However, many others protected only the power of the king over the people. Rulers knew that the best way to maintain their power was to disarm the people–particularly those who posed a threat to their rule.

In the United States, the controversy over firearms and the first federal gun control legislation didn't really begin until the early 1900s. Since that time, more than 20,000 gun control laws have been enacted in the United States at federal, state, and local levels.

The issue of whether gun control laws really work is hotly contested. Some people believe gun control laws keep guns from falling into the wrong hands and thereby prevent violent crimes. Others insist that criminals will simply find other ways to obtain weapons, and gun control laws only prevent law-abiding citizens from exercising their right to own guns.

As you read about the federal gun control laws passed since the turn of the century, see if you agree with these laws. If so, what other laws, if any, do you think should be passed?

Gangsters and Sawed-Off Shotguns

In the early 1900s, new industries and sprawling urban areas began to grow rapidly. As people flocked from farms and the wide-open spaces of the country to crowded cities, social tensions increased.

By the 1920s, a new phenomenon hit the streets–gangsters who toted every kind of firearm from sawed-off shotguns to automatic weapons. You've probably seen gangsters portrayed in movies. Usually one gang pulls out machine guns in a local restaurant and blasts away at another gang while innocent customers dive for cover. Although somewhat exaggerated, these images are not too far from the truth. As people felt their safety threatened, some Americans began to question whether people had the right to carry firearms. Others thought there was a greater need than ever for private citizens to be able to protect themselves.

In response, Congress passed the Miller Bill in 1927. One of the first major federal gun control bills in the United States, it banned the sale of concealable firearms through the mail. Seven years later, Congress enacted the National Firearms Act of 1934. The new law required people who bought sawed-off shotguns, rifles, shotguns with barrels less than 18 inches (46 centimeters) long, fully automatic firearms, and silencers to register the firearm and pay a tax on it. All of these firearms were commonly used by gangsters. But Congress didn't stop there. Only four years later, it passed the Federal Firearms Act of 1938, which established licensing and record-keeping procedures for gun manufacturers, dealers, and importers involved in interstate commerce (selling and transporting guns from one state to another). It also prohibited mailing firearms to known criminals.[2]

Then, as now, some people applauded these new laws and saw them as necessary to protect their safety. Other people, however, opposed any type of firearms regulations and saw these efforts as the first of many steps to deny citizens the right to own firearms. By 1959, there was an even split among Americans on this subject. In a Gallup Poll (a poll known for its surveys of public opinion) conducted at that time, 50 percent of those surveyed said they felt handguns should be outlawed except for police use.[3]

Assassinations and Rising Crime Rates

Thirty years later, in 1968, Congress passed the next federal gun control law in response to specific events that took place during that decade.

The sixties were turbulent years. Three events in particular shook the nation to its roots—the assassinations of President John F. Kennedy, civil rights leader Martin Luther King, Jr., and presidential candidate Senator Robert Kennedy. These tragedies gave new force to the movement for gun control laws.

You may have seen scenes on television or in movies of people protesting the Vietnam War during the 1960s. There were also demonstrations against segregation, and President Lyndon Johnson declared a War on Poverty. Movements for social and political changes abounded. At the same time, crime rates were skyrocketing.

One of the outcomes from this social turmoil was the Gun Control Act of 1968, which strengthened the Federal Firearms Act of 1938. The 1968 Gun Control Act limits the sale of firearms from foreign exporters, manufacturers, and dealers to U.S. importers, manufacturers, and dealers. Second, it bans the importation from other countries of some handguns, such as "Saturday Night Specials"–defined by Handgun Control, Inc. as guns that have a barrel length of less than three inches (7.6 centimeters). Third, it prohibits individuals from purchasing handguns from a state they do not live in and requires that only dealers can sell long guns from state to state. Also, sales must be in compliance with the laws of the dealer's and buyer's home states. Fourth, it creates a separate penalty for individuals caught using a firearm while committing a federal crime.[4] And, finally, in an effort to prevent firearms from falling into the hands of the wrong people, it restricts certain people from purchasing firearms. The restricted groups include:

- minors (under 21 for handguns and under 18 for rifles and shotguns);
- convicted criminals;
- drug addicts;
- persons who have been judged to be mentally incompetent;
- persons dishonorably discharged from the military;
- persons who have renounced (given up) their U.S. citizenship;
- illegal aliens; and
- fugitives from justice.[5]

President John F. Kennedy, top left, moments before he was shot and killed while riding in a motorcade in Dallas, Texas. His wife, Jacqueline, and Governor John Connolly are riding with Kennedy. Center, Jack Ruby, a Dallas nightclub owner, shot and killed Lee Harvey Oswald, who was accused of shooting John Kennedy, while Oswald was in police custody. Below, Robert F. Kennedy was shot and killed while campaigning for the presidency.

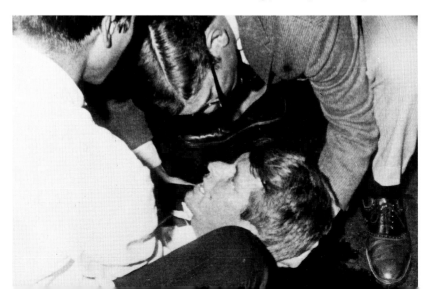

Shocked aides pointed toward the source of the shot that killed Martin Luther King, Jr.

Opponents of gun control believe the 1968 law takes away their right to keep and bear arms—a right that they think the federal government should not be able to regulate. Proponents of gun control laws see the Gun Control Act of 1968 as a definite step in the right direction. However, both groups generally agree that the act does not succeed in keeping guns out of the hands of criminals.

One of the perceived flaws in the Gun Control Act of 1968 is that it requires purchasers to sign a legal document stating that they do not belong to any of the restricted groups (listed on page 48). Dealers, however, are not required to check whether or not the individual is telling the truth. Basically, it is an honor system. But someone who is buying a gun to commit a crime will probably not hesitate to lie when filling out a legal document.

Recent events offer many examples to support this problem with the Gun Control Act of 1968. In August 1987, for example, Larry Dale went into a gun shop in Tulsa, Oklahoma, lied about his criminal record, and purchased a handgun. Twenty-four hours later, he walked into a grocery store across the street from where he had purchased the weapon and opened fire. One man was killed, and another was injured.[6] In October 1987, Arthur Kane, a convicted criminal, also lied on the purchase form to obtain a handgun. Forty-five minutes later he shot and killed his stockbroker in South Miami, wounded another individual, then killed himself.[7]

Other loopholes in the Gun Control Act of 1968 are apparent. The act does little to regulate the transfer of firearms from one person to another, for example. Even if convicted criminals choose not to lie when filling out the purchase document, they can simply ask a friend to buy a gun for them. Also, while the act banned the importation of some foreign-made handguns, it did not restrict the importation of handgun parts. Once the law was enacted, manufacturers immediately began importing the necessary parts from overseas and assembling the handguns in the United States. This loophole was closed in 1986, when the importation of handgun parts was prohibited. However, according to Susan Whitmore of Handgun Control, Inc., U.S. manufacturers have now begun to manufacture these guns in the United States.

While gun control supporters call for tighter restrictions (more laws to close such loopholes), opponents insist that gun control laws don't work. We don't need more gun control laws, they argue. We need better *enforcement* of laws that control the criminal.

The Last Decade

Not all gun control legislation works to tighten gun con-

This type of handgun is commonly called a "Saturday Night Special."

trol regulations. In 1986, Congress passed the Firearms Owners' Protection Act, also known as the McClure-Volkmer Act. Although this act strengthens firearm misuse penalties dealing with certain violent and drug-related crimes, it decreases penalties for other gun violations in lesser crimes. The act also weakens some of the restrictions of the Gun Control Act of 1968. For instance, it allows the interstate sale of rifles and shotguns, provided the sale is within the laws of both states, and reduces federal licensing and record-keeping requirements for dealers. In addition, the Firearms Owners' Protection Act allows the interstate transportation of firearms if the firearms are not loaded and not readily accessible–easy to get to and use.[8]

In 1989, President George Bush took a step toward further regulation of firearms. By executive action (an act or regulation initiated by the president), he banned the importation of 43 models of foreign-made, military-style assault rifles. Based on a study conducted by the Bureau of Alcohol, Tobacco and Firearms, he claimed that these weapons were not suitable for sporting purposes. While some people praised President

Bush's action, others argued that this action further violated their right to bear arms. Many others wondered what purpose the ban will serve since it was based on external features relating to the way a firearm looks. All foreign manufacturers had to do to bypass the law was to change some of the features on the banned firearms, according to Handgun Control, Inc. Also, since assault weapons are manufactured in the United States, American manufacturers simply picked up the slack by increasing production of those types of weapons.

Gun control advocates call for a complete ban on the manufacture of all military-style assault weapons in the United States, according to Whitmore. Since many gun control supporters believe these weapons are designed for

In Miami, Florida, Dade County medical examiners remove one of two bodies from a brokerage office, where disappointed investor Arthur Kane opened fire, killing one person and wounding another before killing himself.

combat use, they wonder why law-abiding citizens need them. Many proponents of gun control believe that a complete ban will eventually dry up the pool of assault weapons on the market and make it impossible for criminals to buy such weapons. Opponents of gun control usually disagree with this reasoning. According to NRA spokesperson Allen Hodgkins, a complete ban won't serve any useful purpose, since criminals will find a way to get the weapons whether there's a ban or not. Furthermore, many people believe that private citizens should have access to weapons as good as those of the military as a protection against government tyranny.

To close one of the major loopholes in the Gun Control Act of 1968–namely, the honor system mentioned above–new legislation has been proposed, partly because of a single incident. On March 30, 1981, in Washington D.C., John Hinckley pulled a .22-caliber revolver from his pocket and opened fire on President Ronald Reagan, White House Press Secretary James Brady, and two security men. Although he was injured by a bullet that lodged only an inch from his heart, Reagan recovered. Brady was shot in the head and suffered severe brain injury that left him permanently disabled. Hinckley had presented a valid driver's license and purchased his gun for $29 in a Dallas pawn shop. Although he used a false address, at the time of purchase he was not a convicted felon or someone judged to be mentally incompetent.[9]

Some people believe that a waiting period is needed between the time a person applies to buy a firearm and the time when the actual purchase is made in order to do a background check on the buyer. Most gun control supporters say a waiting period and background check would

This was the chaotic scene moments after John Hinckley attempted to kill President Ronald Reagan. The body lying on the right on the sidewalk is Press Secretary James Brady. Police and members of the secret service scramble to capture Hinckley.

prevent many shootings. Sarah Brady, a lobbyist for Handgun Control, Inc. and the wife of James Brady, is one of several people who have worked to get Congress to approve a major gun control bill, commonly known as the Brady Bill, that would require a seven-day waiting period.

On May 8, 1991, the Brady Bill passed by a vote of 239 to 186 in the House of Representatives. The Senate included a slightly different version in its Omnibus Anti-Crime Bill–a bill that addressed not only gun control, but many other issues as well. A joint committee, made up of negotiators from both the House and Senate, passed a compromise version that combined some elements from both the House and Senate bills but eliminated others. The compromise measure, passed by the joint committee on Sunday, November 24, 1991, required a five-day waiting period for handgun purchases. It also set up a program to update criminal records so dealers

Sarah Brady, wife of James Brady and a spokesperson for Handgun Control, Inc.

could eventually conduct instant checks on purchasers through a centralized computer system. After President George Bush threatened to veto the compromise bill, however, it lost many supporters, and Congress abandoned it.

Would a waiting period really protect lives, as proponents have suggested? Would a waiting period have stopped Hinckley? In the *Gun Rights Fact Book*, Alan M. Gottlieb quotes James Baker of the National Rifle Association's Institute for Legislative Action. In testimony before Congress, Baker said:

> [Hinckley] was using a valid Texas driver's license issued May 23, 1979, to make his firearms purchase. The contention that a background check would have "uncovered" the fact that he did not physically reside at the address listed on his license is a willful distortion of the criminal record check made by local police. To the contrary, had a check been run and all criminal records been thorough and completely available, they would have confirmed that Hinckley was not a prohibited person and that his last known address was in Lubbock, Texas.[10]

Some states already have waiting periods for handgun purchases, and officials in many of those states are pleased with the results. The California Attorney General's office, for example, says it caught 1,200 prohibited handgun buyers in one year, and the superintendent of the New Jersey state police says 10,000 convicted criminals have been caught trying to buy handguns in the 20 years since the state required a background check.[11]

Gottlieb, however, feels that any benefits are more than outweighed by the enormous cost of such a procedure. "If the police really wanted to catch the few criminals who do purchase guns from legal sources, they literally would have to spend millions of dollars and thousands of manpower hours investigating the backgrounds of gun purchasers."[12] What's more, our nation's criminal records are in sad disarray. Not only would a criminal check take more than one

Police marched to the U.S. Capital to lobby for the Brady Bill.

month to complete, its reliability, according to the U.S. Attorney General as reported by the NRA's Institute for Legislative Action, would be no better than the toss of a coin because we do not have adequate records on criminals.[13]

An article in *U.S. News & World Report* summed up the situation this way: "Using them [waiting periods] for criminal record checks would prove a logistical nightmare. The idea that the FBI computers keep tabs on every criminal case is a myth. In truth, Justice Department experts acknowledged ... [their] files list 25 million arrests, an 'unknown fraction' of which have led to convictions that render defendants ineligible to buy guns."[14]

What's more, the Department of Justice and Attorney General's Office point out that five-sixths of all criminals currently obtain firearms through unregulated means.[15] The reality is that even if there were an effective way to conduct background checks, criminals could simply buy firearms on the **black market** or steal them. As a result, the National Rifle Association believes that a waiting period and background check would only restrict law-abiding citizens from purchasing firearms when they want or need them.

State Laws

Many people believe that the federal government has no right to enact gun control laws. In their opinion, if gun control laws are necessary, states should have the power to pass their own laws, as they do now. This means that one state can permit anyone to use any type of firearm, while a neighboring state can ban firearms altogether.

The result of differing state gun control laws is a patchwork of laws that vary from one state to another. Proponents of gun control insist that it's time for an effective *national* gun control policy. A single national policy would eliminate the confusion of laws from one state to another. It would also prevent criminals who live in tightly restricted states from buying or transferring firearms from a neighboring state where gun control laws are lax, or not very strict.

Susan Whitmore of Handgun Control, Inc., reports, for example, that more than 90 percent of the handguns used in crime in New York come from states with weak handgun laws. But the National Rifle Association points out that "gun running" is already illegal, and penalties for this activity are provided under the Gun Control Act of 1968. The solution to the problem lies in the enforcement of current laws, not in passing new laws.

Although many laws have been passed at both the state and local levels, there are basically four ways in which states restrict the use of guns:

Registration: Some states require gun owners to report the serial numbers of their guns to the police and notify them if the gun is sold.

Permits: In some states, individuals must obtain a permit before they can purchase a gun. Criminals, drug addicts, and mentally incompetent individuals may be denied a permit, while other people may receive restricted permits, such as the right to keep a gun at a shooting club, but not at home.

License to Carry: Individuals in some states are required to obtain a license to carry their guns whether they carry them openly or conceal them.

Waiting Periods: Some states require gun purchasers to wait up to three weeks before they're able to buy a gun.

State Gun Control Restrictions

STATE	APPLICATION AND WAITING PERIOD	PERMIT TO PURCHASE	REGIS-TRATION	LICENSE TO CARRY OPENLY	LICENSE TO CARRY CONCEALED
ALABAMA	✔			✔	✔
ALASKA				★	⊘
ARIZONA				★	⊘
ARKANSAS				⊘	⊘
CALIFORNIA	✔			★	✔
COLORADO				★	✔
CONNECTICUT	✔			✔	✔
DELAWARE				★	✔
DISTRICT OF COLUMBIA	✔		✔	⊘	⊘
FLORIDA				✔	✔
GEORGIA				✔	✔
HAWAII	✔	✔	✔	✔	✔
IDAHO				★	✔
ILLINOIS	✔	✔	✔	⊘	⊘
INDIANA	✔			✔	✔
IOWA		✔	✔	✔	✔
KANSAS		✔	✔	★	⊘
KENTUCKY				★	⊘
LOUISIANA				★	✔
MAINE				★	✔
MARYLAND	✔			✔	✔
MASSACHUSETTS		✔	✔	✔	✔
MICHIGAN		✔	✔	✔	✔
MINNESOTA	✔	✔	✔	✔	✔
MISSISSIPPI				★	⊘
MISSOURI	✔	✔	✔	★	⊘

Data Sources: U.S. Bureau of Alcohol, Tobacco and Firearms; National Rifle Association; Handgun Control, Inc.

STATE	APPLICATION AND WAITING PERIOD	PERMIT TO PURCHASE	REGIS-TRATION	LICENSE TO CARRY OPENLY	LICENSE TO CARRY CONCEALED
MONTANA				★	✔
NEBRASKA				★	⊘
NEVADA				★	✔
NEW HAMPSHIRE				★	✔
NEW JERSEY	✔	✔	✔	✔	✔
NEW MEXICO				★	⊘
NEW YORK	✔	✔	✔	✔	✔
NORTH CAROLINA		✔	✔	★	⊘
NORTH DAKOTA				⊘	✔
OHIO		✔	✔	★	⊘
OKLAHOMA				★	⊘
OREGON	✔			★	✔
PENNSYLVANIA	✔			✔	✔
RHODE ISLAND	✔			✔	✔
SOUTH CAROLINA				✔	✔
SOUTH DAKOTA	✔			★	✔
TENNESSEE	✔			⊘	⊘
TEXAS				⊘	⊘
UTAH				⊘	✔
VERMONT				⊘	⊘
VIRGINIA		✔	✔	★	✔
WASHINGTON	✔			✔	✔
WEST VIRGINIA				✔	✔
WISCONSIN	✔			★	⊘
WYOMING				★	✔

✔ = Required   ★ = Legal, no license required   ⊘ = Not Applicable (conduct banned)

Children at Cleveland Elementary School mourn their classmates who were killed when Patrick Edward Purdy opened fire with an AK-47 assault rifle in the schoolyard in 1989.

FIREARMS
AND SOCIETY

On a cool day in January 1989, many children ran around the playground at Cleveland Elementary School in Stockton, California. They were making the most of the little time they had left to play before the bell rang, signaling the beginning of afternoon classes.

While the children were playing, Patrick Edward Purdy entered the schoolyard with a Chinese-made AK-47 assault rifle. Dressed in army fatigues, he opened fire on the unsuspecting children and continued firing for seven minutes. In newspaper reports, teacher Lori Mackey said she first thought the sounds she heard from the playground were fireworks exploding. But when she looked out the window, she saw children scattering in every direction. She could hear their screams from where she stood. Five children were killed that day, and 29 other children and one teacher were wounded before Purdy took one final shot and killed himself.

The Stockton case was not an isolated incident. A similar occurrence took place in 1988 at Hubbard Woods Elementary School in Winnetka, Illinois, a suburb of Chicago. Laurie

Dann entered the school, shot one child in a bathroom and 5 children in a classroom. One of the children died. One adult was also shot and killed during the course of Dann's escape. Stories about gun-related deaths fill the newspapers every day. Such stories are one of the reasons many Americans favor tighter gun control laws. It's time to put an end to this madness, gun control advocates say, by reducing the number of privately owned weapons–particularly assault weapons and handguns–in the United States. If these firearms were made less available to the public, they believe, there would be fewer gun-related crimes and **homicides** as well as fewer fatal accidents and suicides.

Why the focus on handguns and assault weapons? Because handgun crimes represent 27 percent of all violent crimes by armed offenders (during the period from 1979 to 1987)[1] and 46.8 percent of all homicides (during the period from 1980 to 1987)[2]. Assault weapons, on the other hand, are becoming the favored weapon of criminals, especially of drug gangs, says Susan Whitmore of Handgun Control, Inc.

According to Handgun Control, Inc., every 2½ minutes someone is injured by a handgun in this country[3] Each year between 1979 and 1987, handguns were used in an average of 639,000 violent crimes. During this same time frame, criminals used handguns to kill an average of 9,200 people and wound 15,000 others each year.[4]

Although the number of injuries and deaths from assault weapons like the one used by Patrick Purdy is not as high, the toll is still alarming. The use of assault weapons in crime rose more than 78 percent between 1987 and 1988.[5] And, although assault weapons account for a very small percentage of all firearms (currently there are only about one

24

Some people enjoy using semiautomatic weapons, such as the AK-47 above, for recreation.

million semiautomatic assault weapons on the streets in the United States), they are used in 1 out of every 10 gun-related crimes, according to governmental data compiled by Cox Newspapers. Because most police are still armed only with standard six-shot revolvers, police are clearly in much greater danger as they confront these well-armed criminals.

But will more gun control laws reduce gun-related crime, accidents, and suicides? This question forms the heart of the gun control debate.

If Guns Are Outlawed . . .

America–the land of the free and the home of the brave–is different in many respects from other countries. The U.S. economic system, its military might, and the "American Dream" (in which every person, regardless of his or her background, can succeed) are some of the things that set the U.S. apart. But when it comes to violence and the use of firearms, it is harder for U.S. citizens to hold their heads high.

In 1988, 7 people were murdered with handguns in Great Britain, 8 in Canada, 13 in Australia, 25 in Israel, and 53 in Switzerland. In the United States, however, the number of victims murdered by handguns totalled 8,147.[6]

While some people argue that the United States is simply a more violent culture, proponents of gun control argue that the primary difference between "us" and the "other guys" is the ease with which we are able to obtain guns in this country. They may have a point. Firearms are strictly regulated in all the countries mentioned above, with the exception of the United States.

Australia: A background check and license to possess a handgun are required. Licenses are usually granted only to businesses for security or to gun clubs for target shooting.

These weapons, collected by the police, demonstrate how well armed criminals are. Do police and private citizens need similar weapons to defend themselves?

British police, called bobbies, do not carry guns.

Canada: Handguns must be registered and purchasers must obtain a permit for possession of a handgun. Purchasers are carefully screened through a background check.

Great Britain: Handguns can be bought only for sport and usually must be kept at a gun club. A certificate is required for the purchase of a handgun.

Israel: Licenses are required to carry, possess, or buy a handgun. Thorough background checks, including personal interviews, are required.

Switzerland: Handgun laws require a background check, a permit to purchase a handgun, and handgun registration.[7]

Looking at this global picture suggests that gun control laws do indeed work: countries with tighter gun control laws have fewer homicides. But sometimes there is more to a picture than immediately meets the eye. Even though the United States far surpasses other countries in murders committed with handguns, opponents of gun control say this has little to do with the fact that other countries have tighter laws. Many of those opposed to gun control believe it can be explained by cultural differences between those countries and the United States. Some people think that because of the "Wild West" history of the United States, perhaps it is more violent than other countries. Australia, however, also has a "wild" history.

Also, criminal penalties are not as severe in the United States as those in other countries. According to the National Rifle Association, most foreign countries are two to six times more effective in solving crimes and punishing criminals than the United States is.[8]

As reported in the July 31, 1989, issue of *U.S. News & World Report*, "the differences in crime can be attributed to American revolving-door justice. In a typical year in the United States, there are 8.1 million serious crimes like homicide, assault, and burglary. Only 724,000 adults are arrested and fewer still (193,000) are convicted. Fewer than 150,000 adults are sentenced to prison, with 36,000 serving less than a year."[9]

This lax criminal justice system, opponents of gun control argue, is one of the reasons that the United States has higher crime and homicide rates than any other country. Simply stated, criminals in the United States feel they can commit crimes without fear of being caught or severely punished.

In a telephone interview, NRA spokesperson Allen Hodgkins said, "Let's quit confusing gun control with crime control. They're not the same thing. To think passing one more gun control law in a country where we already have 20,000 gun laws to deter criminal activity will solve the problem is absurd. Of all the gun control laws enacted in the past quarter century, not one city or state has experienced a reduction in crime rates in comparison to its neighboring cities and states without such laws. We need to control the criminal through a tougher criminal justice system–not the weapons these criminals use."[10]

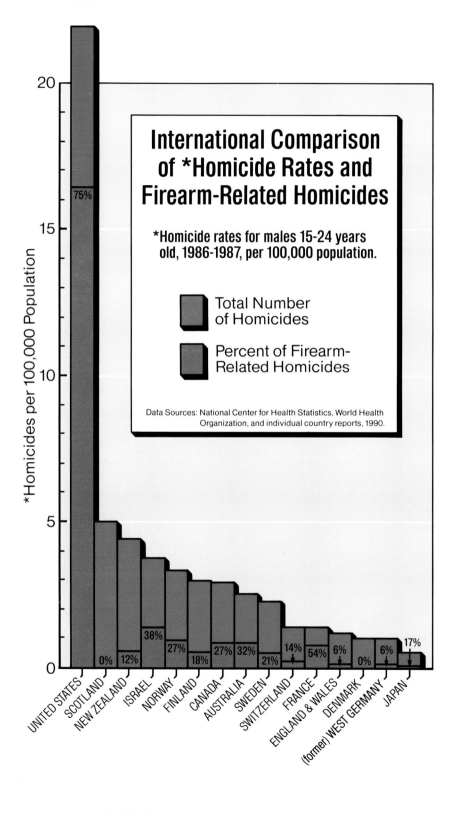

Many people relate the wide-spread ownership and use of guns to the "Wild West" history of the United States.

While gun control laws may not reduce crime rates, as pointed out by Hodgkins, one of the few studies conducted on this topic suggests that tighter laws may reduce the rate of homicide. A study in the New England Journal of Medicine compared two cities on opposite sides of the American/Canadian border–Seattle and Vancouver.[11] Both have very similar populations, rates of unemployment, income levels, cultural values, and justice systems. In fact, the top nine network television programs in Seattle are the same as the top nine programs in Vancouver.[12] Between 1980 and 1986, both cities had similar rates of burglary, assault, and robbery. The rate of assaults involving firearms, however, was seven times higher in Seattle than in Vancouver.

Because the only apparent difference between the two cities was stricter gun control laws in Vancouver, the study concluded that restricting access to handguns may reduce the rate of homicide in a community. Attacks with guns more often end in death than attacks with other weapons, such as knives. If criminals did not have such easy access to guns, chances are there would be fewer murders–even if the crime rate remained the same.

However, the National Rifle Association says that if guns are outlawed, only outlaws will have guns. A criminal is by definition, someone who disobeys laws.[13] "No serious person believes that [gun control laws will be effective enough] to keep guns out of the hands of organized crime, professional criminals, or well-connected terrorists and assassins," according to the National Rifle Association.[14] It's the law-abiding citizens who suffer. Criminals will still be able to obtain firearms, but law-abiding citizens will not have that option for self-defense.

What's more, the NRA says, gun control laws won't work because Americans are not ready to give up their guns. When the government prohibited the use of alcohol in the 1920s and 1930s, it didn't stop the demand for alcohol in the United States. The American people, for the most part, still wanted a sip of beer, a martini, or a gin and tonic after a hard day's work. Bootleggers made a fortune selling the then-illegal beverages on the black market to fill the demand. Although no one has proposed totally outlawing guns in this country, the National Rifle Association says restrictive gun control laws won't work any better than prohibition of alcohol did in the early part of this century. Such laws will only make a black market in guns more profitable.[15]

The National Rifle Association also opposes Handgun Control, Inc.'s proposal to totally ban the sale of assault weapons in the United States. First of all, according to the NRA,

Many private citizens believe they must carry a gun to protect themselves from potential assailants.

"semiautomatic, military-style rifles, including the M1, M-14, and the Colt AR-15, are used in hundreds of sanctioned, high-power shooting tournaments each year. Hundreds of thousands of individuals use these rifles for recreation.[16] More importantly, how will authorities get the three to four million assault weapons out of the hands of Americans who already own them? Guns can last centuries with minimum care, and merely cutting off the supply will have little or no effect for generations.[17]

Susan Whitmore, of Handgun Control, Inc., knows that new laws aren't going to affect the large number of assault weapons currently on the streets in this country. "But we want to stop it at that level," she says, "before it proliferates into 30 or 300 million." Handgun Control, Inc. opposes a very small class of semiautomatic weapons that come equipped with combat hardware, which, according to Whitmore, distinguishes them as assault weapons. "These are pieces of equipment that are not used by hunters or sports enthusiasts," she says. "They're things like pistol grips, which enable the shooter to spray-fire from the hip, flash suppressors, and large-capacity magazines of 20 to 100 rounds of ammunition. It's against the law in most states to hunt with over five or ten rounds. So, clearly these weapons do not serve legitimate sporting purposes."

But the NRA disagrees. "All of the accoutrements [accessories] that make these firearms appear sinister are merely cosmetic," says Hodgkins. "And most were developed to make the firearms used by soldiers easier to handle and use. These weapons should not be banned based on their cosmetic appearance. *How* one uses a gun defines whether or not it is a legitimate purpose. Not *what* one uses."

Self-Protection or Potential Tragedy?

It was the first day of summer vacation for 12-year-old Joseph Bixler. He and his brother played in their home in Oceanside, California, with a new "toy" they had found in the house–their father's handgun. The gun fired accidentally, and on that summer day in 1988, Joseph Bixler was shot and killed by his 13-year-old brother.

It wasn't an unusual incident. Gunshot wounds to children ages 14 and under are the fourth leading cause of accidental death among children in the United States.[18] In fact, it is estimated that gunshot wounds to children ages 16 and under have increased 300 percent in major urban areas since 1986. One out of every 25 children admitted to American pediatric trauma centers suffers from such

Children often mistake real guns for toys.

wounds, according to Barbara Barlow, M.D., in a press release from the American Academy of Pediatrics, Committee on Trauma, Surgical Section.[19]

"Basically, there are three reasons why children are being shot," says Barlow. "First, there are more guns in homes. In fact, most accidental shootings are done by other children. Second, children are shot by stray bullets–bullets not meant for them. And then, there are children who are shot intentionally by other children over drug deals."[20]

In most cases, however, the hundreds of deaths and injuries that occur each year among children are accidents caused by guns kept in the home.[21] According to proponents of gun control, handguns in the home are a magnet for children, who too often mistake them for toys. If the guns were unloaded and locked up, these children would be alive today. Everyone agrees that Americans need to be educated about gun safety.

Does that mean people shouldn't keep guns in their homes? Let's look at another story. Susan Benson (whose name has been changed to protect her identity) was asleep in her bed. Suddenly she was awakened by the sound of breaking glass downstairs. She heard footsteps and was certain someone was in her house. She lived alone and didn't know what to do. She reached for the telephone to call the police, but just then a large man with a gun burst through her bedroom door, ripped the telephone from her hand, and started to choke her with the cord. It was too late to do anything, and Susan became the victim of violence, rape, and yet another homicide. If she had had a gun in her nightstand, she might have been able to defend herself.

Rising crime rates and fear of assault have intensified feelings among many Americans that they need to protect themselves. According to the National Rifle Association, 58 percent of handgun owners in America own handguns primarily for this purpose.[22] An armed citizen–or even the threat of an armed citizen–they believe, is the most effective deterrent to crime in this nation. Some research supports this belief. Professors James Wright and Peter Rossi, coauthors of the U.S. Justice Department's three-year study of weapons and criminal violence in America, questioned more than 1,800 felons on this topic and found that 85 percent would attempt to find out if a potential victim were armed before committing a crime. Fifty-three percent of these felons did not commit a specific crime for fear that the victim was armed.[23]

According to the NRA "in areas having lower levels of private firearms ownership, the robbery rates are almost invariably higher because criminals are aware that their

As violence in the United States increases, more and more women feel the need to own a gun.

intended victims are less likely to have the means with which to defend themselves."[24] Many NRA members believe that it was the clear intention of the framers of the Constitution that citizens be able to protect themselves. They argue that private citizens should be able to use all modern firearms for such purposes.[25]

But Handgun Control, Inc. argues against keeping firearms in the home for protection. First, most burglaries occur when no one is at home.[26] Even if the victim were at home, would he or she have time to get to the weapon to use it in defense? Second, every year, at least 150,000 handguns are stolen from the homes of law-abiding citizens.[27] According to the Center to Prevent Handgun Violence, many are later used in violent crimes by drug addicts, drug pushers, and gang members. Third, what will happen as criminals arm

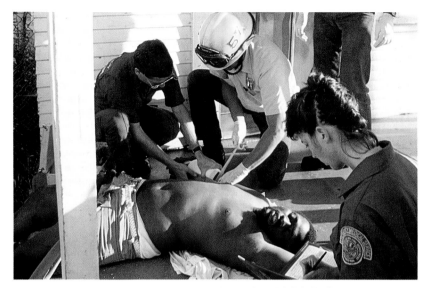

Guns can turn fist fights into gun fights, in which injuries are more serious and deaths are more likely. This man was the victim of a drive-by shooting.

themselves with more powerful, deadly weapons, such as assault rifles? Will police forces and citizens increase their own arsenals to keep pace and protect themselves? The NRA believes that they should be able to and that it is their right to do so.

But Susan Whitmore of Handgun Control, Inc. asks, "What happens when we come down to a society where everyone is armed to the teeth? Commonplace fistfights and arguments will turn into gunfights. We saw that in California a couple years ago when people were being shot and killed over fender benders. Had people not had quick and easy access to these weapons, lives would have been saved. The bottom line is that if we really believed more guns made us safe, we'd be the safest country in the world. And we're far from that."

Finally, and most importantly, it is commonly believed that loaded guns in the home can create a danger for the people who live there. According to a recent study in the *New England Journal of Medicine*, a gun in the home is 43 times more likely to be used to kill a family member or friend than to to kill an intruder.[28] One study looked at all gunshot deaths that occurred in King County, Washington, from 1978 through 1983. The researchers found that of the 398 deaths that occurred in residences where firearms were kept, only 2 deaths involved an intruder shot during attempted entry. Seven persons were killed while trying to defend themselves.

Furthermore, for every homicide that occurred in self-defense involving a firearm kept in the home, there were 37 suicides and 1.3 accidental deaths. "Keeping firearms in the home carries associated risks," according to the article. "These include injury or death from unintentional gunshot wounds, homicide during domestic quarrels, and the ready availability of an immediate, highly lethal means of suicide."[29]

The use of handguns for suicide is a growing problem. In 1970, about 33 percent of the suicides by women between the ages of 15 and 24 were committed with guns, while 42 percent were committed with drugs. But in 1984, more than 50 percent were committed with guns, and only 19 percent were committed with drugs. The suicide rate among adolescents has tripled in the past three decades, making suicide the third leading killer of teenagers[30] after automobile accidents and homicides.[31] Nearly 3,000 teens use handguns to commit suicide every year. Guns are the most deadly suicide method—nine out of ten attempted suicides involving handguns are completed.[32]

According to the Western Psychiatric Institute and Clinic and the University of Pittsburgh Graduate School of Public Health, a suicidal teenager living in a home with an easily accessible gun is more likely to commit suicide than a suicidal teenager living in a home where no gun is present. The reason for this is that most teen suicides are impulsive, with little or no planning, and 70 percent occur in the victims' homes.[33]

Will more gun control laws reduce the number of suicides? NRA spokesperson Allen Hodgkins argues that if someone has decided to commit suicide, he or she is going to do it whether or not there's a gun in the home. Many other methods, such as knives and pills–which are often readily available–will simply take the place of guns, he said. The problem is not guns; the problem is the suicidal person who no longer sees a reason to live.

But according to Susan Whitmore, spokesperson for Gun Control, Inc., guns kill instantly, unlike pills and knives. If a suicide is attempted with something other than a gun, someone may find the victim before the suicide attempt actually becomes fatal. Or, should the victim have a change of heart, he or she would probably have one last chance to call for help.

However, Hodgkins of the NRA asks why suicide rates are lower in the United States than in many countries, such as Japan, where guns are severely restricted? It's a good question.

Is the Problem Guns or People?

During the Vietnam War, 58,000 American soldiers, marines, sailors, and airmen were killed; during that same time period, more than 70,000 people in the United States were killed by guns –mostly handguns.[34] In 1987, 8,413 Ameri-

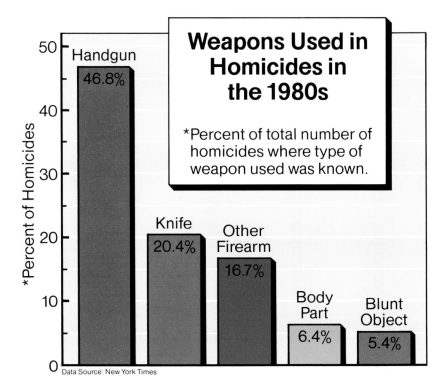

Data Source: New York Times

cans were murdered with handguns, and 1,200 were killed by accident.[35] An additional 12,671 people committed suicide using a handgun.[36]

Are guns the problem or are people the problem? The question is not easily answered. Psychologists, public interest groups, and congressional committees have filled volumes trying to find the answer. Obviously, if people (such as criminals and suicidal individuals) are the problem, we need to focus our attention exclusively on them, with tougher prison sentences and better mental health programs. Firearm safety training programs, many of which have been initiated by the National Rifle Association, will help tremendously in reducing the number of accidental gun-related deaths in the United States.

But when it comes to homicide, there can be little dispute that guns are indeed one of the most deadly weapons available. Proponents of gun control believe that–in addition to tougher prison sentences–what's needed are better mental health programs and firearm safety training programs. They believe that restricting the ownership of firearms will save lives. Easy access to firearms in the United States, in their opinion, makes killing too easy.

Nonetheless, the question remains: Will gun control laws help prevent incidents like the one that occurred at Cleveland Elementary School? Or will they only interfere with the rights of law-abiding citizens who use firearms for recreation and/or self-protection against criminals?

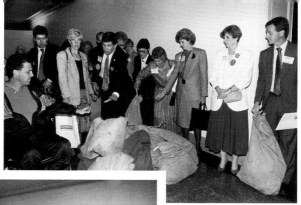

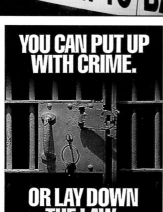

Citizens on both sides of the gun control issue communicate their points of view to the government. Clockwise from top, gun control advocates delivering petitions to the House of Representatives, Brigadier General Joe Foss (former NRA president), a gun victims' demonstration at the Capitol, an NRA poster, members of the National Coalition to Ban Handguns lobbying before a congressional committee

PUBLIC OPINION: AMERICA'S GUIDING FORCE

When the founders of our government drafted the Constitution that would govern the United States for centuries, they had one goal in mind: they wanted the government to draw its power from the people, not the other way around. To them, "the people" were the government, and what "the people" wanted as a group would be the law of the land.

That's why public opinion is so important in this country. Although you may not always agree with the results, you've seen how public opinion influences change. For example, just about every state in the nation has strengthened its penalties for drunken driving in the last 10 years because "the people" wanted it that way. When people began to voice their opinions about smoking in public places, laws governing where and when an individual could smoke gradually became more strict to reflect "the people's" changing attitude.

So what do Americans think about gun control? The numbers from many polls and surveys on the subject should tell the story. But they don't. As with all the other aspects of the gun control debate, people on both sides disagree once again–this time about the validity of surveys that don't support their point of view. Let's take a look at a few polls and surveys conducted recently.

Polls and Surveys

In a 1989 Gallup Poll, 70 percent of those polled said they felt laws governing the sale of firearms in general should be made more strict, while only 6 percent said laws should be less strict and 22 percent felt they should remain unchanged.

In the same poll, 72 percent favored federal legislation banning the manufacture, sale, and possession of semiautomatic assault weapons, while only 23 percent were against such legislation.

Of those polled, 91 percent favored a national law requiring a seven-day waiting period before a handgun could be purchased.

In a 1989 survey conducted by Yankelovich Clancy Shulman for *Time* and CNN (Cable News Network), 84 percent of those polled said they thought that violence from the use of guns is becoming a bigger problem in the United States these days. Five percent felt it was less of a problem and seven percent saw no difference.

But, in one of its publications, the National Rifle Association says, "It is a fact that most people do not know what laws currently exist; thus, it is meaningless to [say] that people favor 'stricter' laws when they do not know how 'strict' the laws are in the first place." The NRA publication goes on to say that unbiased, scientific polls have consistently shown that most people (1) oppose registration of firearms; (2) oppose giving police the power to decide who should own guns; and (3) do not believe that stricter gun laws will prevent criminals from illegally obtaining guns.[1]

Bernhard Goetz shot and wounded four youths on a New York subway when they approached him to ask for money. Many people viewed his action as heroic. But was he protecting himself or unfairly attacking the youths?

In a 1989 survey of officers in state, county, and local police agencies, 90 percent said they did not believe banning firearms (handguns, shotguns, or rifles) would reduce criminals' ability to obtain such weapons, and 71 percent said they did not believe a waiting period would have any effect on criminals getting firearms.[2]

In the same survey, 69 percent said they believe law-abiding citizens should have the right to purchase any type of firearm for sport or self-defense under state laws that now exist, and 88 percent did not believe that banning the private ownership of firearms would result in fewer crimes from firearms.[3]

Given the differences in the results of public opinion polls, it is difficult to draw any definite conclusions about what sort of gun control laws Americans want—or don't want. But one thing is certain. More and more people are taking sides in this debate. The laws and regulations governing gun control will reflect the views of the side with the strongest voice.

APPENDIX

Taking a Stand

What do you think about gun control? To help formulate an opinion, see if you can answer the following questions based on what you have read and how you feel about guns. If your answer to most of the questions listed below is (a), chances are you favor some form of gun control. If your answer is most often (b), there is a good chance you see little reason to enact more gun control laws.

(a) Although guns have long been a part of our American heritage, with the development of more powerful, deadly weapons, it's time to limit the use of guns in our society.
(b) Guns have been a part of our American heritage for everything from hunting to protecting the free state; they should continue to be not only part of our heritage but also of our future.

(a) A seven-day waiting period for handgun purchasers to receive their firearm would reduce violence by (1) allowing an angry purchaser time to cool off before obtaining a weapon and/or (2) allowing officials to conduct a background check on the individual to ensure that he or she does not have a criminal record.
(b) Requiring a seven-day wait to purchase a handgun violates a constitutional right of individuals to keep and bear arms.

(a) Private ownership of guns promotes violence.
(b) Private ownership of guns prevents violence because it deters criminals.

(a) Since most people killed by guns are shot by someone they know, the benefits of having a gun in the home do not balance the risks.
(b) People need guns to protect themselves against criminals.

(a) Teen suicides are impulsive for the most part and guns are deadly weapons. Fewer suicides, especially among teens, would occur if guns were less available.
(b) People who want to commit suicide will do so whether or not guns are available.

(a) Fewer gun-related accidents would occur if guns were less available.

(b) The availability of guns does not cause gun-related accidents. Fewer gun-related accidents would occur if children and adults were taught better firearm safety.

(a) The sale of military-style assault weapons should be banned because they are quickly becoming the favored weapon of criminals. They serve little hunting or recreational purpose.

(b) The Second Amendment clearly indicates the right to own firearms for the efficiency of a well-regulated militia. Automatic and semiautomatic military-style firearms can certainly be used for that purpose. Private citizens should therefore be able to own such firearms.

(a) Limiting the availability of firearms will reduce the number of gun-related crimes and/or homicides in this country.

(b) Criminals will find a way to obtain firearms illegally if firearms are made less available. Reducing the availability of firearms will not reduce crime or homicide.

(a) Guns kill; because they are one of the most deadly weapons a person can use, we should develop tougher penalties for people who use guns illegally and limit the availability of firearms.

(b) Guns don't kill, people do. To reduce crime and/or homicide, attention should be focused on developing tougher penalties for people who use guns illegally.

After reading about the gun control debate, you may have formed your own opinion on the issue. It may be time for you to take a stand and voice your opinion in the debate. People like you and your friends will decide this issue. The most direct way to voice your opinion is to write to your senator, your congressional representative, or the president. If you're not sure of your legislator's name, call your library or your local chapter of the League of Women Voters. Here are a few rules to remember when you write:

- Write on stationery. Be sure to put your signature above your name if you have typed it.

- Put your return address on the letter–envelopes are easily lost.

- Ask your legislator to let you know his or her position on gun control. You're entitled to a clear answer to your question.

- When writing to the President, address your envelope: President _____, 1600 Pennsylvania Avenue N.W., Washington, D.C. 20500. Begin your letter with "Dear Mr. President."

- When writing to your senator, address your envelope: The Hon. _____, United States Senate, Washington, D.C. 20510. Begin your letter with "Dear Senator _____."

- When writing to your congressman or congresswoman, address your envelope: The Hon. _____, House of Representatives, Washington, D.C. 20515. Begin your letter with "Dear Congressman or Congresswoman _____."

- You can telephone your senator or member of Congress by dialing (202) 224-3121 and asking for the individual by name. The operator will transfer your call to the office you request. You can call the White House to express your opinion by calling (202) 456-1414 or (202) 456-1111. These will be long-distance calls.

- Handgun Control, Inc., 1225 Eye Street, N.W., Suite 1100, Washington, D.C. 20005, 202-898-0792.

- National Rifle Association, 1600 Rhode Island Avenue, Washington, D.C. 20036, 202-828-6000.

There are many other ways to get involved. You can get books on gun control and gun care and safety at your local library. Organize a group in support of your position at school to learn more about the issues. Invite speakers from one or both sides to participate. You can find speakers through your local law enforcement agency, a local NRA chapter, Handgun Control, Inc., or a local gun control advocacy group. Become involved. The debate will be won in the public arena.

Endnotes

INTRODUCTION

[1] Arthur L. Kellerman, M.D., and Donald T. Reay, M.D., "Protection or Peril? An Analysis of Firearm Related Deaths in the Home," *The New England Journal of Medicine* 314 (1986): 1557-60.

[2] National Rifle Association Institute for Legislative Action, *NRA Firearms Fact Card 1990* (Washington D.C., 1990), brochure.

[3] Kellerman and Reay.

[4] *Washington Post,* 19 November 1987.

[5] S. P. Baker, B. O'Neill, and R. S. Karpf, *The Injury Fact Book* (Lexington, MA: Lexington Books, 1984).

[6] Joseph A. Fernandez, Superintendent, Dade County Public Schools, *Kids + Guns: A Deadly Equation* (Miami, Florida, 1989).

[7] Center to Prevent Handgun Violence, *Facts about Teen Suicide and Handguns* (Washington, D.C., May 1990), brochure.

[8] League of Women Voters of Minnesota, *Facts and Issues: The Sale, Use, and Possession of Firearms in Minnesota* (St. Paul, January 1990), 5.

[9] Handgun Control, Inc., *Membership Brochure* (Washington, D.C.).

[10] National Rifle Association Institute for Legislative Action, *National Rifle Association Annual Report* (Washington, D.C., 1989), 18, 23.

[11] National Rifle Association Institute for Legislative Action, *Ten Myths about Gun Control* (Washington, D.C., June 1990), brochure.

[6] Susan Whitmore, Handgun Control, Inc., phone interview with author, June 1990. All further attributions to Whitmore are based on this interview.

CHAPTER 1. GUNS IN A BRAVE NEW WORLD

[1] Stephen P. Hallbrook, *That Every Man Be Armed* (Albuquerque: University of New Mexico Press, 1984), 62.

[2] David T. Hardy, *Origins and Development of the Second Amendment* (Southport, CT: Blacksmith Corporation, 1986), 64.

CHAPTER 2. THE SECOND AMENDMENT

[1] *United States v. Cruikshank,* 92 U.S. 542 (1875).

[2] Ibid.

[3] *Presser v. Illinois,* 116 U.S. 252 (1886).

[4] *Miller v. Texas,* 153 U.S. 535 (1894).

[5] *United States v. Miller,* 307 U.S. 174 (1939).

[6] National Rifle Association Institute for Legislative Action, *The Right of the People to Keep and Bear Arms* (Washington, D.C., July 1990), 12-15.

[7] Ibid., 14.

[8] Whitmore interview.

[9] Ibid.

[10] Hallbrook, 169.

[11] Whitmore interview.

[12] Hallbrook, 169.

[13] Michael R. Rand, *Handgun Crime Victims, A Department of Justice Statistics Special Report* (Washington, D.C., June 1990), 1.

CHAPTER 3. GUN CONTROL LAWS

[1] Laws of Alfred, *I English Historical Documents c. 500-1042*, ed. D. Douglas (1968), Sec. 7 at 375; Sec. 38.1 at 379; Secs. 19-19.2 at 376; Sec. 19.3 at 376.

[2] League of Women Voters of Minnesota, *Facts and Issues*, 1.

[3] Lee Kennett and James Laverne Anderson, *The Gun in America: The Origins of a National Dilemma* (Westport, CT: Greenwood Press, 1975), 225.

[4] Ibid., 243-244.

[5] League of Women Voters of Minnesota, *Facts and Issues*, 3.

[6] Minnesota Association for Crime Victims, *Newsletter, Special Issue*, August 1985.

[7] Ibid.

[8] League of Women Voters of Minnesota, *Facts and Issues*, 3.

[9] National Rifle Association, *Facts Against the "Waiting Period" Frenzy*, brochure.

[10] Alan M. Gottlieb, *Gun Rights Fact Book* (Bellevue, WA: Merril Press).

[11] Minnesota Association for Crime Victims, *Newsletter*.

[12] Gottlieb, 91-92.

[13] National Rifle Association Institute for Legislative Action, *Twelve Tall Tales* (Washington, D.C., 1990), 4.

[14] "Nibbling the Bullet on Gun Control," *U.S. News and World Report*, 4 December 1989, 14.

[15] National Rifle Association Institute for Legislative Action, *Twelve Tall Tales*, 4.

CHAPTER 4. FIREARMS AND SOCIETY

[1] Rand, 1.

[2] "More Americans Are Killing Each Other," *New York Times*, 31 December 1989, 20.

[3] Handgun Control, Inc., *Fact Card*, brochure.

[4] Rand, 1.

[5] Jim Stewart and Andrew Alexander, "Assault Weapons Muscle in on the Front Lines of Crime," *Firepower: Assault Weapons in America*, 21 May 1989, 1 (newspaper).

[6] League of Women Voters of Minnesota, *Facts and Issues*, 4.

[7] Ibid.

[8] National Rifle Association Institute for Legislative Action, *Ten Myths*, 9.

[9] "Victims of Crime," *U.S. News and World Report*, 31 July 1989, 16-19.

[10] Allen R. Hodgkins, National Rifle Association, phone interview with author (Washington, D.C., June 1990). All further attributions to Hodgkins are based on this interview.

[11] "Handgun Regulations, Crime, Assaults, and Homicides: A Tale of Two Cities," *The New England Journal of Medicine*, 10 November 1988, 1256-1262.

[12] Seattle local market TV ratings, 1985-1986. (Based on Arbitron television ratings.) Provided by KING-TV, Seattle, Washington. Vancouver local TV ratings, 1985-1986. Provided by Bureau of Broadcast Measurement, Toronto.

[13] National Rifle Association Institute for Legislative Action, *Ten Myths*, 20.

[14] B. Bruce-Briggs, *The Great American Gun War* (Washington, D.C.: National Rifle Association Institute for Legislative Action, 1976), 51.

[15] Hodgkins interview.

[16] National Rifle Association Institute for Legislative Action, *Ten Myths*, 12.

[17] Bruce-Briggs, 52.

[18] Center to Prevent Handgun Violence, *Facts About Kids & Handguns* (Washington, D.C., May 1990), brochure.

[19] American Academy of Pediatrics, *Children Shooting Children: A Serious, Growing Problem* (Elk Grove Village, IL, 18 October 1988), press release.

[20] Ibid.

[21] Center to Prevent Handgun Violence, *Child's Play, A Study of 266 Unintentional Handgun Shootings of Children* (Washington, D.C.), 1-2.

[22] National Rifle Association Institute for Legislative Action, *NRA Firearms Fact Card*, 4.

[23] National Rifle Association Institute for Legislative Action, *Ten Myths*, 5.

[24] Ibid., 19.

[25] Ibid., 13.

[26] Handgun Control, Inc., citing FBI Uniform Crime Report (Washington, D.C., 1987).

[27] Handgun Control, Inc., citing *Firearm Abuse: A Research and Policy Report* (Washington, D.C.: Police Foundation, 1977).

[28] Kellerman and Reay, 1557-60.

[29] Ibid., 1557.

[30] Center to Prevent Handgun Violence, *Facts About Teen Suicide & Handguns* (Washington, D.C., April 1989), brochure.

[31] Ibid.

[32] Ibid.

[33] Ibid.

[34] "Retired Justice Powell: No Constitutional Right to Own Handguns," *Washington Post*, 8 August 1988.

[35] Handgun Control, Inc., *Fact Card*.

[36] National Center for Health Statistics (Washington, D.C.).

CHAPTER 5. PUBLIC OPINION: AMERICA'S GUIDING FORCE

[1] National Rifle Association Institute for Legislative Action, *Ten Myths*.

[2] National Association of Chiefs of Police, *American Law Enforcement Officers Survey for 1989* (Washington, D.C.), 1-2.

[3] Ibid.

Glossary

appeal: in a court case, the right of the losing party to ask that the case be reconsidered by a higher court; to take a case or proceeding to a higher court for decision. A person who loses a case in either a federal court of appeals or in the highest state court may appeal to the Supreme Court.

black market: a place where goods are illegally bought and sold

circuit court of appeals: a federal appellate court, or court of appeals. The United States is divided into 12 circuits, or districts, each of which has a federal court of appeals.

convicted: to be found guilty of a crime

duck blind: a camouflaged place made with reeds and perhaps canvas or cloth. Hunters construct duck blinds to conceal themselves from ducks while hunting.

felon: one who has committed a felony, a serious crime

homicide: the killing of one human being by another

illegal aliens: one who resides in another country illegally (without having been granted permission by that country's government)

premeditated: planned and willful

uphold: to agree with, or support

Bibliography

American Academy of Pediatrics. *Children Shooting Children: A Serious, Growing Problem.* Elk Grove Village, IL: American Academy of Pediatrics, Oct. 18, 1988. Press release.

American Law Enforcement Officers Survey for 1989, National Association of Chiefs of Police, Washington, D.C.

Anderson, Jervis. *Guns in American Life.* New York: Random House, 1984.

"Assault Weapons Muscle in on the Front Lines of Crime." *Firepower: Assault Weapons in America*, 21 May 1989.

Baker, S. P., B. O'Neill, and R. S. Karpf. *The Injury Fact Book.* Lexington, MA: Lexington Books, 1984.

Bruce-Briggs, B. *The Great American Gun War.* Washington, D.C.: NRA Institute for Legislative Action, 1976.

Caplan, David I. *Constitutional Rights in Jeopardy.* Washington, D.C.: NRA Institute for Legislative Action.

Center to Prevent Handgun Violence. *Child's Play, A Study of 266 Uninten-tional Handgun Shootings of Children.* Washington D.C.: Center to Prevent Handgun Violence.

_____. *Facts About Kids and Handguns.* Washington D.C.: Center to Prevent Handgun Violence, May 1990.

_____. *Facts About Teen Suicide and Handguns.* Washington D.C.: Center to Prevent Handgun Violence, April 1989.

_____. *Handgun Safety Guidelines.* Washington D.C.: Center to Prevent Handgun Violence, 1988.

Federal Bureau of Investigation, U.S. Department of Justice. *Crime in the United States.* Washington D.C.: Government Printing Office, 1986.

Fernandez, Joseph A., Superintendent, Dade County Public Schools. *Kids + Guns: A Deadly Equation.* Miami, FL: Dade County Public Schools, 1989.

Gottlieb, Alan M., *Gun Rights Fact Book.* Bellevue, WA: Merril Press, 1988.

Greene, D. S. "Gun Control." *Editorial Research Reports,* 13 November 1987.

Hallbrook, Stephen P. *That Every Man Be Armed.* Albuquerque: University of New Mexico Press, 1984.

Handgun Control, Inc. *Fact Card.* Washington, D.C.: Handgun Control, Inc.

_____. *Membership Brochure.* Washington D.C.: Handgun Control, Inc.

_____. *You Can Do Something About Handgun Violence.* Washington, D.C.: Handgun Control, Inc.

"Handgun Regulations, Crime, Assaults, and Homicide: A Tale of Two Cities." *The New England Journal of Medicine* (10 November 1988): 1256-1262.

Hardy, David T. *Origins and Development of the Second Amendment.* Southport, CT: Blacksmith Corporation, 1986.

Kellerman, Arthur L., M.D., and Donald T. Reay, M.D. "Protection or Peril?" *The New England Journal of Medicine* 314 (1986): 1557-60.

Kennett, Lee and James Laverne Anderson. *The Gun in America: The Origins of a National Dilemma.* Westport, CT: Greenwood Press, 1975.

Laws of Alfred, Secs. 7, 19-19.3, 38.1. In *I English Historical Documents c. 500-1042,* edited by D. Douglas, 1968.

League of Women Voters of Minnesota. *Facts and Issues: The Sale, Use, and Possession of Firearms in Minnesota.* St. Paul: The League of Women Voters, January 1990.

Minnesota Association for Crime Victims. *Newsletter, Special Issue.* Minneapolis: Minnesota Association for Crime Victims, August 1985.

National Center for Health Statistics. *Youth Suicide Surveillance.* Atlanta: Centers for Disease Control, 1986.

National Rifle Association. *Facts Against the "Waiting Period" Frenzy.* Washington, D.C.: National Rifle Association.

_____. *NRA Annual Report*. Washington D.C.: NRA, 1989.

National Rifle Association Institute for Legislative Action. *The Right of the People to Keep and Bear Arms*. Washington D.C.: NRA Institute for Legislative Action, July 1990.

_____. *Ten Myths About Gun Control*. Washington D.C.: NRA Institute for Legislative Action, 1990.

_____. *Twelve Tall Tales*. Washington, D.C.: NRA Institute for Legislative Action, 1990.

Rand, Michael R. *Handgun Crime Victims, A Bureau of Justice Statistics Special Report*. Washington D.C.: U.S. Department of Justice, June 1990.

Siegel, Mark A., Nancy R. Jacobs, and Carol R. Foster. *Gun Control: Restricting Rights or Protecting People?* Wylie, TX: Information Plus, 1989.

"Victims of Crime." *U.S. News and World Report*, 31 July 1989, 16-19.

Woods, Geraldine and Harold. *The Right to Bear Arms*. New York: Franklin Watts, 1986.

Wright, James D. and Peter H. Rossi. *Weapons, Crime, and Violence in America, Executive Summary*. Washington D.C.: U.S. Department of Justice, National Institute of Justice, November 1981.

_____. *Armed and Considered Dangerous: A Survey of Felons and Their Firearms*. New York: Aldine Gruyter, 1986.

Wright, James D., Peter H. Rossi, K. Daly, E. Weber-Burdin. *Weapons, Crime, and Violence in America: A Literature Review and Research Agenda*. Washington, D.C.: Government Printing Office, 1981.

Yeager, M., J. D. Alviani, and N. Loving. *How Well Does That Handgun Protect You and Your Family?* Technical Report No. 2, United States Conference of Mayors, Washington D.C., 1976.

Index

Acknowledgments

The photographs and illustrations in this book are reproduced through the courtesy of: Bettmann Archives, p. 24; *Chicago Sun-Times*/Robert A. Reeder p. 39 (top); Collection of the Supreme Court of the United States, p. 36; Department of Defense Still Media Records Center, p. 26 (top); Michael Evans, the White House, p. 55; Handgun Control, Inc., pp. 56, 57, 82 (top); Hollywood Book and Poster, p. 70; King Features Syndicate, Inc., p. 81; Library of Congress, pp. 18, 19, 21, 25; Missouri Department of Conservation/Jim Rathert p. 8; National Coalition to Ban Handguns, p. 82 (bottom, left and right); National Guard, 30; National Portrait Gallery, London, p. 23; National Rifle Association, p. 82 (center, left); National Shooting Sports Foundation, pp. 6 (both), 15, 26 (bottom), 44 (bottom), 76; Religious News Service, pp. 49 (bottom), 50; Reuters/ Bettmann, 31, 67; Mark Richards, p. 77; Jerome Rogers, p. 40; Jim Simondet, pp. 44 (top), 72; Southdale-Hennepin Area Library, Edina, Minnesota, p. 28 (top); Mike Tachney, p. 76; Texas State Library, Archives Division, p. 49 (center); Richard Trombley, p. 65; UPI/Bettmann, 39 (bottom), 52, 53, 62, 66, 82 (center, right), 85; U.S. Army, p. 41; Virginia State Library and Archives, p. 22.